Beware of The Storybook Wolves

Lauren Child

ORCHARD

FOR CHARLIE

{ make sure you keep this book under something heavy }

AND CRESS

{ who knows how to deal with storybook wolves }

ORCHARD BOOKS
338 Euston Road, London NW1 3BH
Orchard Books Australia
Level 17/207 Kent Street,
Sydney, NSW 2000

First published in 2000 by Hodder Children's Books
This edition published in 2012 by Orchard Books

ISBN 978 1 40831 480 7

The right of
Lauren Child to be identi-
fied as the author and
illustrator of this work
has been asserted by
her in accordance with
the Copyright, Designs
and Patents Act, 1988.

Text and illustrations
© Lauren Child 2000

10 9 8 7 6 5 4 3 2 1

Printed in China

A CIP catalogue record
for this book is available
from the British Library

Orchard Books is a division of
Hachette Children's Books,
an Hachette UK company.

www.hachette.co.uk

Little Red Riding Hood

Little Red Riding Hood

*Thank you
to Soren*

**Every night Herb's mother would
read him a bedtime story.**

Sometimes it was about a big wolf who terrified little
girls and their grandmothers with his chilling growl and
his big yellow teeth. You could tell from the picture that
toothpaste had never been on his shopping list.

The story got very nasty in the middle and everybody
nearly came to a sticky end . . . but, by the last page . . .

...it had all turned out well and went happy-ever-afterly.

It was one of Herb's favourites. He particularly liked the back cover that had a picture of a smaller wolf with a patch over one eye and the words:

For a real thrill try reading the story of THE LITTLE WOLF and THE THREE LITTLE PIGS

IT WILL SCARE YOUR SOCKS OFF

"It scared my socks off."
Cinderella

"I couldn't sleep after reading this."
Rumpel Stiltskin

"It was a real thrill reading this story."
A. Woodcutter

Whenever his mother finished this
bedtime story, Herb would say,
"Don't forget to take that book with you!"

And his mother would ask,
"Why?"

"Because there's a wolf in it, of course,"
Herb would say.

Herb's mother
would smile to
herself because
she knew that
storybook wolves
are not at all
dangerous.

One night, just as they were finishing
the wolf story, the telephone rang.
In her hurry, Herb's mother forgot all
about taking the book with her.

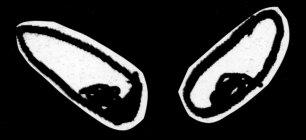

Herb didn't realise
at first but, as he
was snoozing off, he
thought he heard

a
deep
rumbling
sound

coming from his
bedside table.

It was like the
rumbling of
a very
**hungry
tummy**.

Or perhaps even
two very hungry
tummies.

Then he
began to smell a
not-very-nice smell.

A sort of

BAD-BREATH

type of a smell.

Herb got a funny
feeling that two, or
maybe even three, eyes
were watching him.

Unwisely, he
switched on
the light . . .

. . . and there, standing in front of him, was the big storybook wolf and next to him was the other smaller wolf with a patch over one eye. Herb recognised him as the back-cover wolf.

"Mmm," Big Wolf said in a low greedy voice, **"I thought I could smell something tasty. I'm going to gobble you up, little boy."**

And he started to lick his chops.

"Ooh, can I have his little pink toes? They look just like piglets," said Little Wolf.

And he tried to lick his chops, but he wasn't very good at it and just ended up dribbling on the floor.

"I wouldn't eat me yet," stammered Herb, desperately trying to think of a plan to distract the wolves from wolfing him.

"Why not?" said Big Wolf, giving him a sideways stare.

"Yes, why not?" said Little Wolf, trying to give him a sideways stare.

"*Ummm...*
because little boys
are for pudding.
You have to start with
starters, of course."

"I didn't know that,"
said Big Wolf.

"Really?" said Herb, feeling a little bit
pleased with his own craftiness.
"I thought everybody knew that."

"Oh, I knew that," said Little Wolf.

"No, you did not," said
Big Slightly-less-fierce-than-before Wolf.

"Yes, I certainly did," said Little Wolf,
puffing himself up.

"Well, if you're so clever
then what's 'starters'?"
blustered Big Wolf.

You could tell that Little Wolf hadn't even heard of starters but, not wishing to sound stupid, he shouted,

"JELLY is starters! Everybody knows that."

Then Big Wolf and Little Wolf looked at Herb and said,

"Where's the jelly?"

Jelly, jelly, where was a jelly?

Herb's mind was whirring like a frantic thing. Then he caught sight of his book of fairy tales. He had been looking at it last night and it was lying open on the page where the dozy princess falls asleep at her own birthday party.

No one at the table would notice if he borrowed a jelly.

They were all snoozing, tired of waiting for Princess Beautiful to wake up.

Herb was so busy struggling to slide the jelly off the page he didn't notice the **wicked fairy**, wide awake and hiding under the table. She had been listening to every word.

This was bad luck for Herb because the **wicked fairy** hated little boys only slightly less than she hated little girls. They made her very nervous. She'd seen what those little brats, Hansel and Gretel, had done to that poor defenceless witch. Not only did they nibble her cottage half to pieces, but then they went and shoved her in her own oven. Children put her in a very bad mood indeed.

"Oh, you dozy doormats,
   don't you know anything?" snarled the fairy.
"You wolf-half-wits give wickedness a bad name.
   He's tricked you, you twerps:
      little boys are *starters*,
         jelly is pudding."

And with that the wicked fairy jumped back into the book and snapped it shut.

First the wolves went almost purple in the cheeks with embarrassment,

then their eyes went all mean and squinty.

Herb could tell things had taken a turn for the really quite bad.

So he snatched up the fairy-tale book, found the page with the Fairy Godmother and shook it until she tumbled out of the book and on to the floor. She was a bit cross actually because her dress got crumpled and she nearly twisted her ankle.

"Well," she said, "I've got a good mind to turn you into a caterpillar, little boy."

"No, no!" said Herb.
"Don't turn me into a caterpillar;
it's those two who need to be caterpillars."

"Oh no, *not you two again*,"
said the Godmother,

spying the two alarmed wolves.

"Always making
trouble . . .

blowing people's
houses down
and
gobbling
them up
without
so much as a
do-you-mind?"

As she said this she accidentally waved her wand at the little wolf and the smoke went POOF

(just like in the fairy tales)

and

suddenly

there was

"Oh dear, oh dear, this will never do,"
said the Fairy Godmother, shaking her head.
"That dress was meant for Cinderella.
You shook me out of the book just as I was about
to send her to the ball. Awfully nice dress though.
I have an eye for fashion as you can probably tell.
But not at all suitable for a wolf."

he little wolf

standing in a
ballgown.

Little Wolf took one look in the mirror and was so pleased with his new look that he jumped into the fairy-tale book and went to the ball himself.

Which of course left Cinderella having a night in, cleaning the kitchen after all.

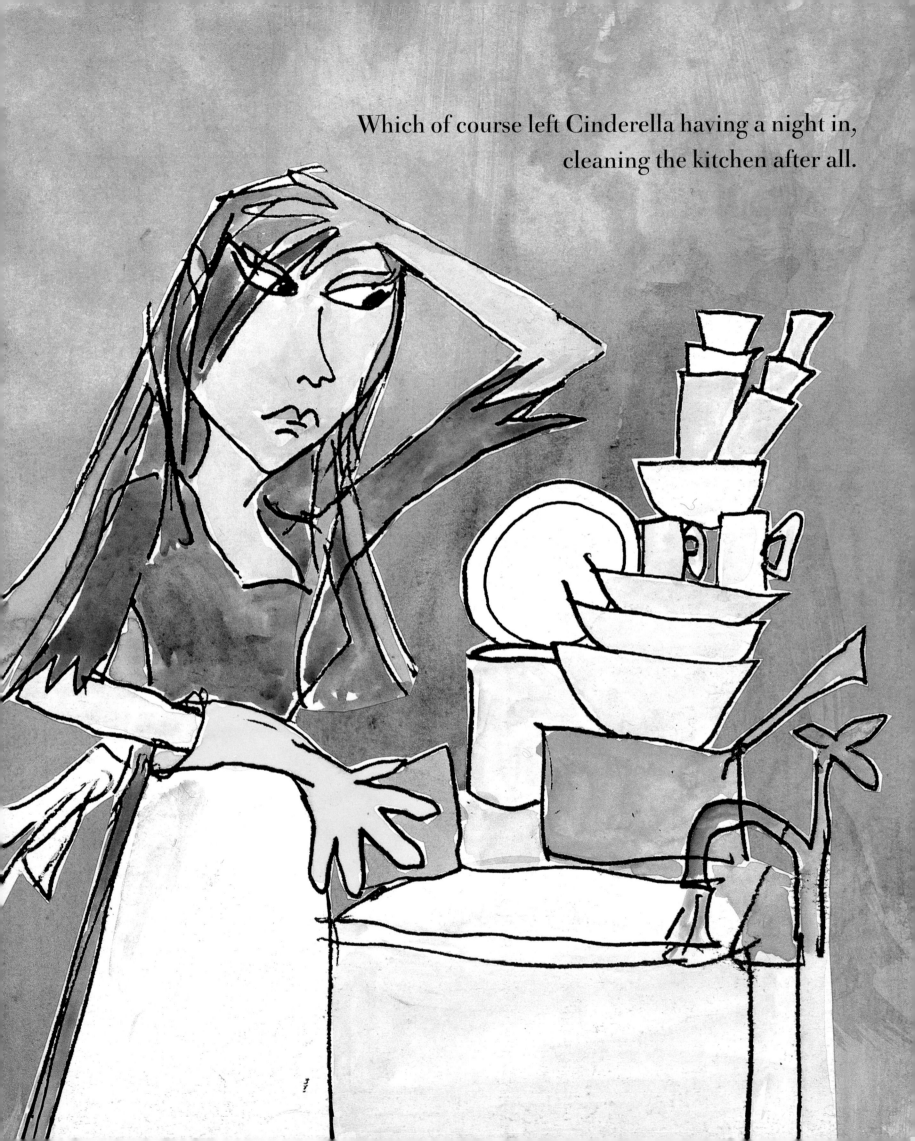

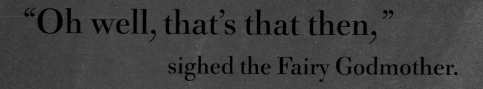

"Oh well, that's that then,"
              sighed the Fairy Godmother.

"I'm not going to be at all popular at the palace now.
I don't know what the king and queen are going to say
when a wolf turns up at the ball to dance with their son.
I imagine they will be very grumpy about it. I do hope
he doesn't start snacking on the guests . . ."

The Fairy Godmother
was so engrossed with
her own problems that
she hadn't noticed that
Big Wolf was poised,
ready to swallow Herb
in one gulp.

"Help!," screeched Herb.

Quick as a quick thing
the Fairy Godmother whooshed her wand
and Big Wolf was just a
tiny caterpillar.

"Oh, I do like caterpillars," said the Fairy Godmother, popping it back in to the wolf storybook. "They're so undemanding. Never bothering me for things, not like frogs, always thinking they are princes. What's more, I really have had enough of being squashed inside a book, doing favours for spoilt princesses. I'm going to take a holiday, somewhere far away from royalty."

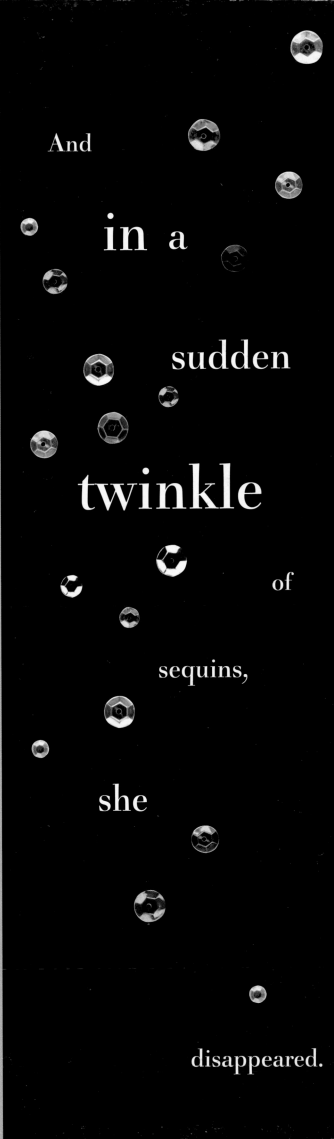

And in a sudden twinkle of sequins, she disappeared.

Before Herb got back into bed he piled up all his books and then put the heaviest thing he could find on top of them, just in case anyone else was tempted to get out of his story.

Then he
SWITCHED OFF
The **LIGHT**
AND DREAMED OF FIERCE
CATERPILLARS
Fashionable Wolves
AND
Grouchy Godmothers

The funny thing was, the next time Herb's
mother came to read the wolf story, there was no wolf
to be seen – just a tiny caterpillar trying with all his
might to terrify a little girl in a red coat.